This Walker book belongs to:

_____

_____

_____

For Becky

First published 2016 by Walker Books Ltd, 87 Vauxhall Walk, London SE11 5HJ

This edition published 2017

2 4 6 8 10 9 7 5 3 1

© 2016 Daisy Hirst

The right of Daisy Hirst to be identified as author and illustrator of this work has been asserted by her in accordance with the Copyright, Designs and Patents Act 1988

This book has been typeset in WB Natalie Alphonse

Printed in China

British Library Cataloguing in Publication Data: a catalogue record for this book is available from the British Library

ISBN 978-1-4063-7313-4

www.walker.co.uk

ALPHONSE, THAT IS NOT OK TO DO!

Daisy Hirst

WALKER BOOKS
AND SUBSIDIARIES
LONDON • BOSTON • SYDNEY • AUCKLAND

ONCE there was Natalie

and then, there was
Alphonse too.

Natalie mostly did not mind there being Alphonse.

They both liked naming the pigeons,

Banana!

Lorraine!

bouncing things off the bunkbeds

and stories in the chair,

and they both loved
making things.

Except that Alphonse did
sometimes draw on the
things that Natalie made,

or eat
them,
and
Natalie
hated
that.

One day when lunch was peas

and telly
was awful

and Mum did not understand,

What a lovely dog!

It is an **HORSE**.

Natalie found Alphonse under the bunkbeds ...

eating her favourite book.

"ALPHONSE, THAT IS NOT OK TO DO!" said Natalie.

Behind the big chair, Natalie drew ...

a tornado,

two beasts,

a swarm of peas

and Alphonse, very small.

but Natalie put her fingers in her ears and went for her bath.

Outside the bathroom,
Natalie heard noises.
She thought she heard ...

"Alphonse? Mum?" called Natalie.
"Alphonse, are you OK?"

It was very quiet.

Natalie opened
the door.

"Natalie, I only tried to get the sticky tape down," said Alphonse, "so I could fix your book.

Only I couldn't reach it, so I tried to suck it down with the hoover,

ROAR!

then I got the chair to stand on, but I sort of ran over the cat,

SCREEEECH!

then I climbed up, but everything fell on my head and then so did the marbles."

Skitter!

Ting!

Dink!

"Are you hurt?" said Natalie.

"No," said Alphonse. "I'm sorry I ate your book."

"It's OK," said Natalie. "I'm sorry I was mean."

"I finished your picture," said Alphonse.

Natalie thought it was ...

Most Excellent Fantastic!

So they had better draw quite a few more.

ALSO BY DAISY HIRST:

978-1-4063-6552-8

978-1-4063-6331-9

 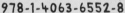